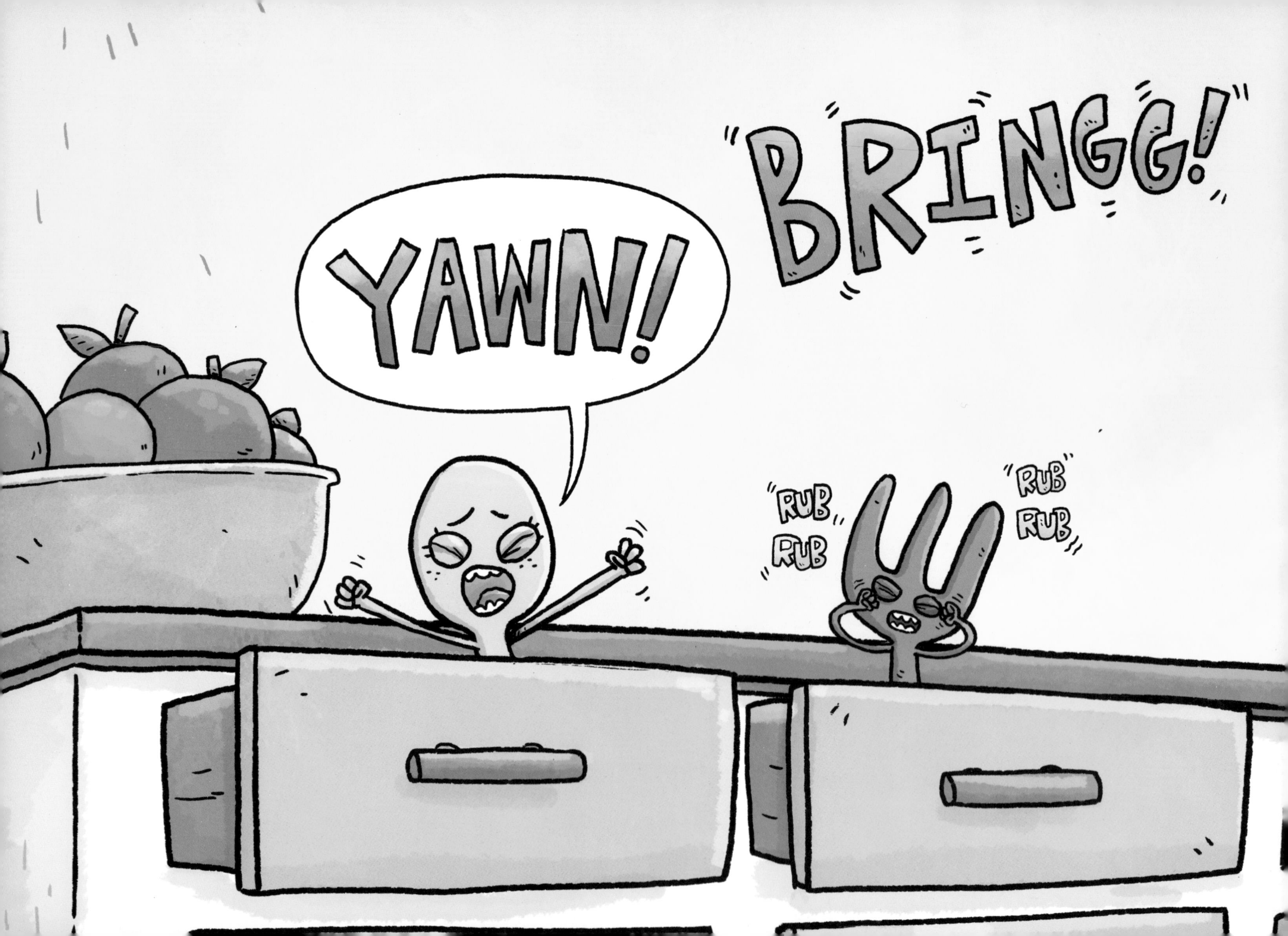
YAWN!
BRINGG!
RUB RUB
RUB RUB

Tiny Spoon vs. Little Fork

Story by
Constance Lombardo

Pictures by
Dan & Jason

Hippo Park

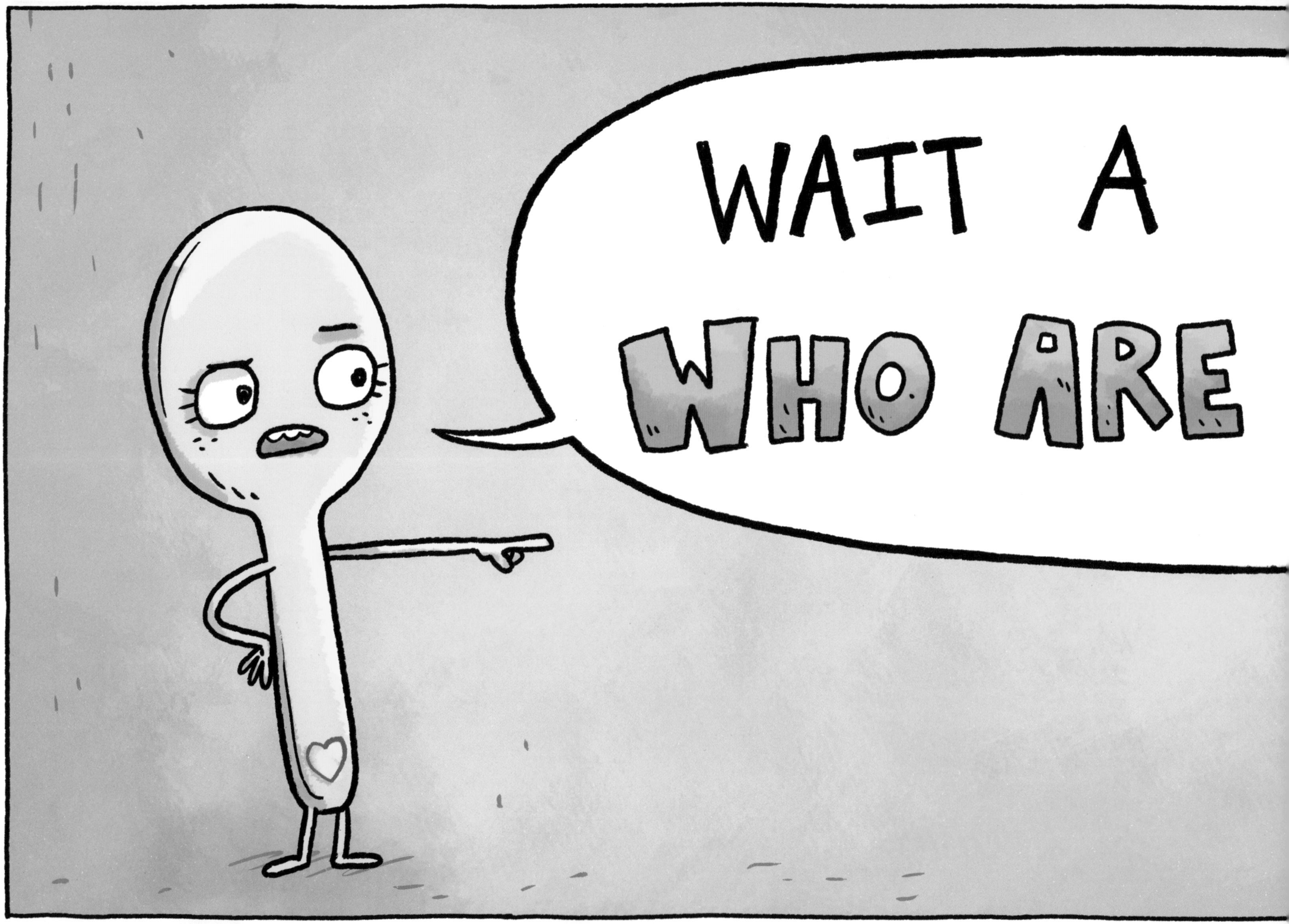
WAIT A
WHO ARE

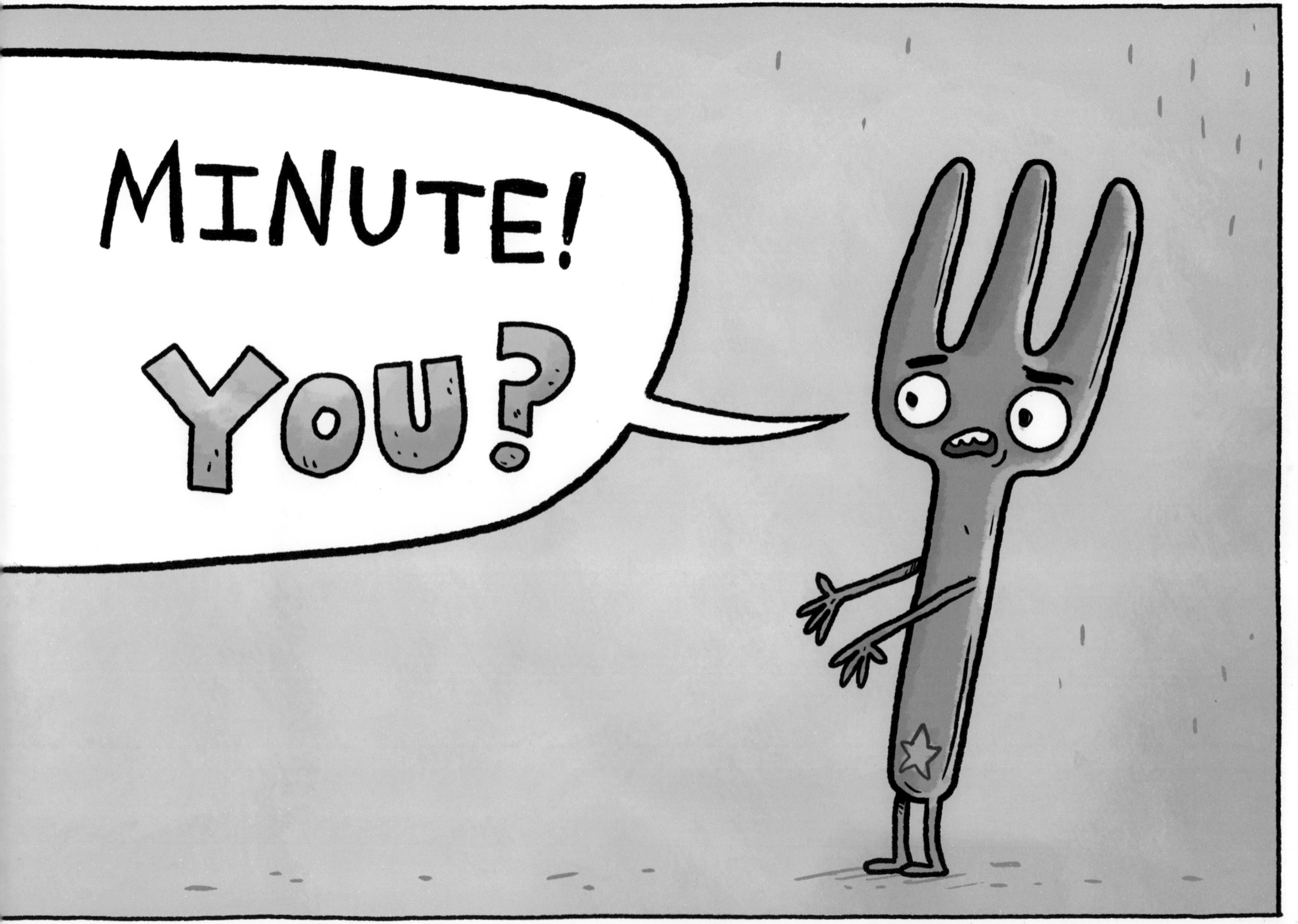
MINUTE!
YOU?

AUNT SOUP SPOON

Dishes up chowder, broth, and tomato soup with love.

DADDY SERVING SPOON

Ladles pasta, stew, and fruit salad with a smile.

COUSIN TEASPOON

Stirs together tea and sugar from morning till night.

GRANDPA SCOOP

Empties ice cream cartons top to bottom before you can say "fudge ripple."

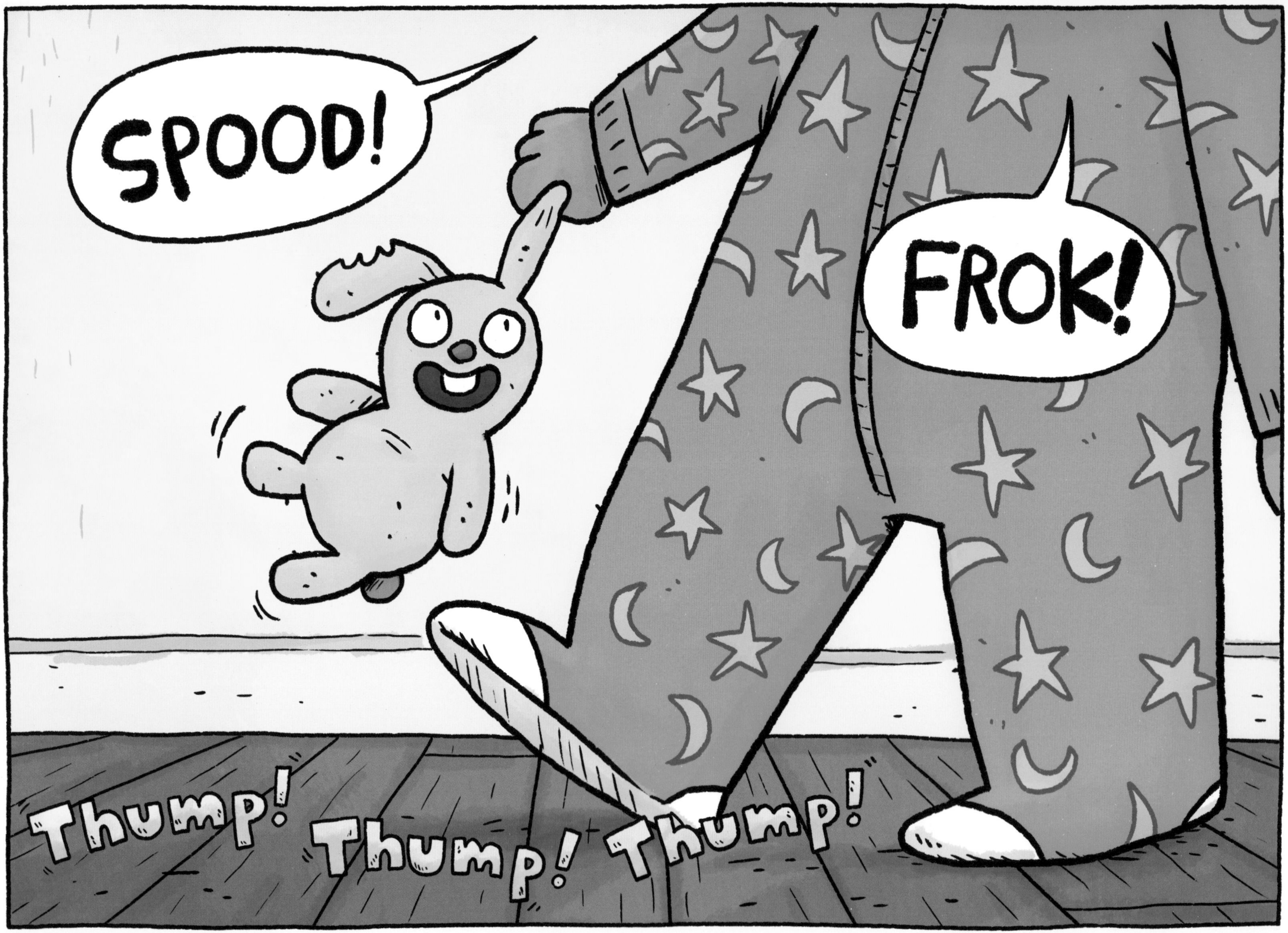
SPOOD!
FROK!
Thump!
Thump!
Thump!

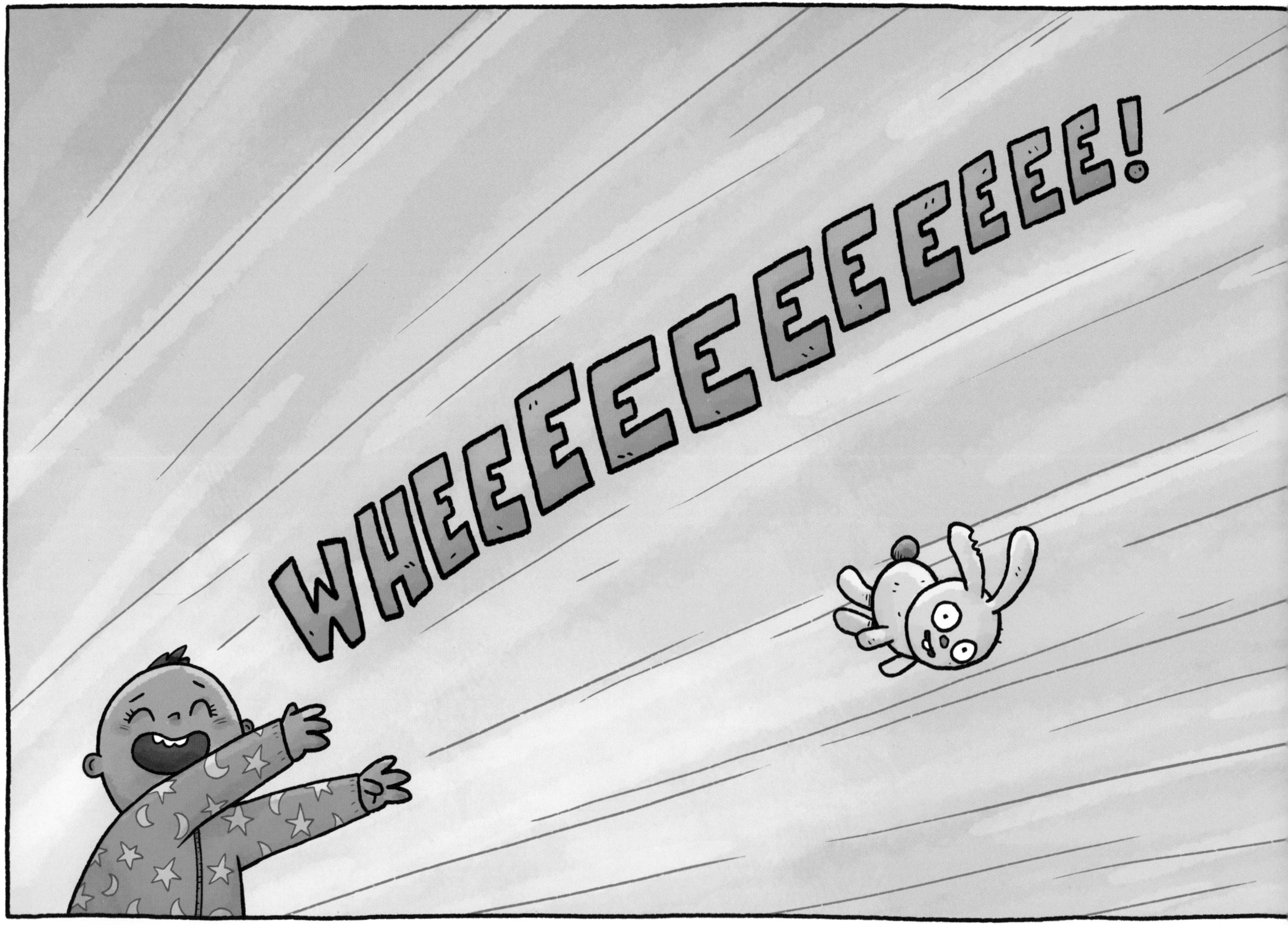
WHEEEEEEEEEEEE!

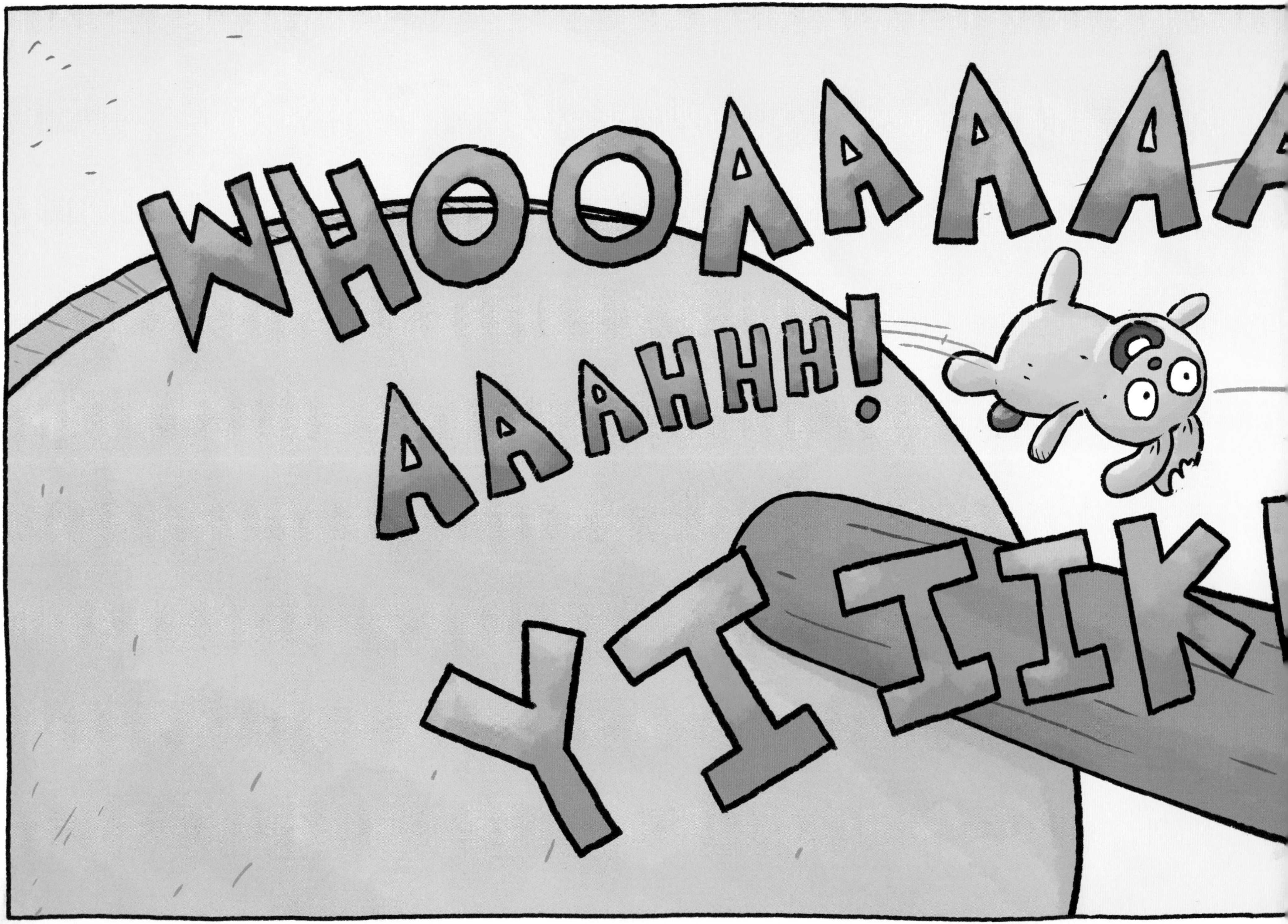
WHOOAAAAA
AAAHHH!
YIIIK

zzz zz z²

For Concetta Lombardo—
an enchanting storyteller,
an amazing cook,
and the perfect grandmother.
　　　　　　　　　—C. L.

We dedicate this book to all the
kids who read and draw comics
at the dinner table.
　　　　　　　　　—Dan & Jason

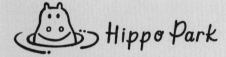 Hippo Park

An imprint of Astra Books for Young Readers, a division of Astra Publishing House
astrapublishinghouse.com
Printed in China

ISBN: 978-1-6626-4006-3 (hc)
ISBN: 978-1-6626-4007-0 (ebook)
Library of Congress Control Number: 2021922637

First edition

10 9 8 7 6 5 4 3 2 1

The illustrations are done digitally.
Typeset in Barb.